Frida María

A STORY OF
THE OLD
SOUTHWEST

Deborah Nourse Lattimore

VOYAGER BOOKS

HARCOURT BRACE & COMPANY

San Diego   New York   London

Requests for permission to make copies of any part of the work should be mailed to:
Permissions Department, Harcourt Brace & Company, 6277 Sea Harbor Drive,
Orlando, Florida 32887-6777.

First Voyager Books edition 1997
Voyager Books is a registered trademark of Harcourt Brace & Company.

Library of Congress Cataloging-in-Publication Data
Lattimore, Deborah Nourse.
Frida María: a story of the Old Southwest/Deborah Nourse Lattimore.—1st ed.
p.   cm.
Summary: Because she does not sew, cook, or dance like a "proper señorita," Frida cannot
please her mother until she saves the day at the fiesta with her special talent.
ISBN 0-15-276636-7
ISBN 0-15-201515-9 (pbk.)
[1. Sex role—Fiction. 2. Southwest, New—Fiction.] I. Title.
PZ7.L36998Fs   1994
[E]—dc20   93-17250

C E F D B

Printed in Singapore

The paintings/illustrations in this book were done in Winsor & Newton watercolors
and Berol Prismacolor pencils over a hand-applied layer of modeling paste on 140-pound
D'Arches hot-press watercolor paper.
The display type was set in Gando Ronde Script by Thompson Type, San Diego, California.
The text type was set in Goudy Village by Thompson Type, San Diego, California.
Color separations were made by Bright Arts, Ltd., Singapore.
Printed and bound by Tien Wah Press, Singapore
This book was printed on Leykam recycled paper, which contains more than 20 percent
postconsumer waste and has a total recycled content of at least 50 percent.
Production supervision by Warren Wallerstein and Pascha Gerlinger
Designed by Lori J. McThomas

With lots of love to
Nicholas and Isabel and Linda Zuckerman
and a salute of appreciation for
Leo Politi and his pueblo,
La Ciudad de Nuestra Señora de Los Angeles

—D. N. L.

It was one month before Fiesta, and Frida María de
Guadalupe y Vega could hardly wait.

Frida's papá made out the invitations.

Frida's mamá was to prepare the food and the decorations.

Marta and Mercedes, Frida's sisters, practiced their dances and songs.

And Tío Narizo, who was a very old *caballero* and Frida's favorite uncle, trained riders from all over the *rancho*, because on the last day of Fiesta there was to be a great horse race.

"Do you think I could ride Diablo at Fiesta?" Frida asked her uncle.

"We will have to ask your mamá, my little fox," Tío Narizo replied.

Frida skipped inside the *hacienda*. She found Mamá sewing the last stitches on her Fiesta dress.

"All fine ladies know how to sew, Frida *mija*," said Mamá. "You have watched long enough. See if you can finish this trim while I go see to the kitchen."

Mamá gave Frida a needle and thread. She was gone a long time. When she finally walked in the door dressed for dinner with Papá, Frida said, "Surprise!"

"Aah!" Mamá shouted.

"Can I wear these when I ride Diablo during Fiesta?" asked Frida.

"No, no," said Mamá. "I can see you have been spending too much time with the horses and your old uncle Narizo. You will just have to wear your purple dress. There is not time to sew you another."

"I'm sorry, Mamá," Frida said.

Mamá put her arms around Frida.

"The time has come for you to behave like a proper *señorita*. Riding Diablo at Fiesta is not the way to do it. Tomorrow I would like you to spend all day inside with Cook."

Indeed, the next morning Frida was in the kitchen. Cook pushed and pulled and punched the dough.

"Like this," said Cook. "*Ay!* How quickly you learn! Your mother will be proud."

Frida rolled and twisted the dough until it stretched from one end of the counter to the other. Then she piled it up and waited for Mamá to come.

"Cook tells me what a good job you are doing," Mamá said as she came in.

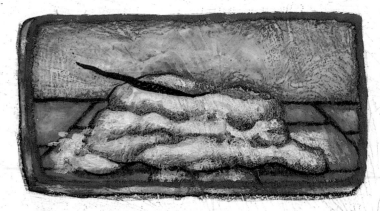

At that very instant a rat ran across the floor.

"Aha!" shouted Frida. She scooped up the dough and threw it like a *reata*. The soft dough landed on the rat.

"*Ole!*" shouted Cook.

"No, no, NO!" cried Mamá. "This is not done!"

Frida helped clean up and followed her mother to the patio.

"I am sorry, Mamá," said Frida. "I did roll the dough the best I could."

"Yes, Frida," said Mamá. "But to throw it across the room! You should not be so wild."

She watched Frida spread her skirt to sit down.

"Now *that* is ladylike," said Mamá. "I am going to ask your sisters to show you how to dance and sing for the Fiesta. I think that is the answer."

Soon Marta and Mercedes had their costumes on and were dancing the *jarabe*. Mercedes played the guitar, too, and Frida tapped her feet with them.

"Isn't this fun, Frida?" asked Marta. "And look, Mercedes, how well Frida does turns! I'll go get Mamá. This will make her happy to see."

But by the time Mamá came in, Frida was loudly stamping

her feet, clapping her hands over her head, and shouting
"Hí-jo-le!" at every turn, just like a *vaquero*. Mercedes was
laughing and strumming her guitar as fast as she could.

"She's really good, isn't she, Mamá?" said Mercedes.

"Enough! Enough!" said Mamá. "This is not proper! You
cannot dance at Fiesta like this. What will Don Ramón and his
snippy wife Doña Tita say?" And she walked out.

Frida sat down in the patio and did not even notice her sisters' kisses as they left. All she could think of was Mamá and Fiesta. She could not sew, she could not cook, she could not dance. Mamá didn't like anything she did. And Mamá did not want her to ride Diablo. Frida tried to take a deep breath, but all she could feel was hot, dry Santa Ana wind sticking to her throat. The patio was quiet, and she was all alone.

For the next few weeks, Frida was very ladylike. She did everything the way Mamá wanted, even though it made her sad. Thinking about Fiesta only made it worse.

Then, FIESTA! Everyone ate the wonderful food.

Everyone danced under paper decorations and ribbons.

Mercedes and Marta sang and played guitar.

Frida sat on the stairs and watched.

Mamá walked past fanning herself. "Come," she said to
Frida. "I hate to see you unhappy. Come out with me to meet
Don Ramón and his wife in the garden."

Frida squeezed her mamá's hand. Don Ramón and Doña
Tita were just outside. Papá and Tío Narizo were there, too.

"I look forward to the great race," said Don Ramón. "No one has ever beaten my horse, Furioso."

"Furioso? The best horse?" exclaimed Tío Narizo. "Perhaps in Monterrey. But in this *pueblo* Diablo has never been beaten!"

"Foolish old man." Don Ramón sniffed. "If your horse moves as quickly as you do, I have already won! I like this so much, I'll bet my horse against yours in the race. The loser will pay the other's city taxes for one year."

"Done!" cried Tío Narizo.

"Oh, no!" said Mamá, waving her handkerchief.

"And I am no fool!" shouted Tío Narizo, grabbing Diablo's reins.

"Stop!" Mamá said, dropping her handkerchief.

The *vaqueros* saw her handkerchief drop and thought it was the signal for the race to begin. They mounted their horses.

In the dust and confusion the riders galloped off. Don Ramón, on Furioso, was in the lead. Tío Narizo, who always moved slowly, was still trying to get his foot into the stirrup.

Frida wrenched her hand free from Mamá's, leapt onto
Diablo, and chased after the others.

Around the mission they went, around city hall, the old
church, and the stores, the *haciendas*, the gardens, and the
cactus. In her mind Frida could hear Mamá saying "Oh! How
unladylike!" but she kept going.

The dust clouds broke open along the home stretch. Frida could see that only she and Don Ramón were still in the race. Neck and neck, they came right at the crowd.

Then, with a great lunge, Diablo flew across the finish line.
Cook, the maids, Marta and Mercedes, Papá and Tío Narizo
were shouting, cheering, screaming, and jumping up and
down. *"Viva Frida! Viva!"*

In the blur of faces, Frida could not see Mamá. Then she did.

"I'm sorry, Mamá." said Frida. "I got my dress very dirty and dusty. I disobeyed you. And I am not a proper señorita."

Mamá threw her arms around Frida.

"You were wrong to disobey me, but I have been very wrong about you. True, you are not the kind of proper señorita I was raised to be. But you are the best Frida there ever was, and I am proud of you. And you have made this—"

"—the best Fiesta ever!" shouted Frida. *"Hí-jo-le!"*

AUTHOR'S NOTE

WHEN I WAS GROWING UP IN SOUTHERN CALIFORNIA, I FOUND NOTHING MORE exciting than to pretend I was a famous *caballero* riding a high-spirited horse along the *Camino Real*, the King's Royal Road. My grandmother, who loved local history and lore, had told me stories about the *ranchos* of the Old Southwest, and many years later, when I wrote *Frida María*, I remembered the story of a famous horse race in 1842, when José Sepulveda (from Los Angeles) and Pío Pico (from San Diego) pitted their horses and their towns against each other. The stakes were very high: the loser had to give the winner 2,000 head of cattle, 1,000 horses, a *rancho* of thousands of acres, and the prize horses competing that day. (Los Angeles won!)

In the pictures of *Frida María*, you will glimpse examples of the art and architecture from each of the missions established by the Franciscan missionary Padre Junípero Serra beginning in 1769 and completed by other members of his order in 1823. These missions—churches and outbuildings and way stations that dotted the western edge of California from the Bay of San Diego to the Bay of San Francisco—still stand today. Early Native Americans, *Californios*, soldiers in the service of King Carlos III of Spain, and many priests and travelers came and went along the *Camino Real*, often stopping at the missions.

Having researched what it might have been like to live then, I have added Frida María and her family to this historical setting. Although it is not likely that a young girl would have raced with the *alcaldes* (mayors of Los Angeles and San Diego), it is not entirely impossible. Perhaps there *was* a Frida María—a young person who took a chance and won. I like to think so.

When you read this story—and see a chocolate whisk hanging from a rack in the kitchen or hear a fountain splashing noisily in the courtyard—perhaps you will also be able to imagine the scent of flowers and the texture of rough pavements or cool, polished tiles beneath your feet. Perhaps you will catch sight of another time when an adventurous girl or boy jumped on a fiery steed and galloped into the hot and dusty Santa Ana winds along the *Camino Real*.

—D. N. L.

GLOSSARY

alcalde   mayor of a city or chairman of the town council

caballero   (ca-bah-YEH-ro)   gentleman; horseman; nobleman

Californio   native of early California

don   title, meaning gentleman

doña   title, meaning lady

fandango   a lively Spanish dance

hacienda   a large estate with a main house, stables, and outbuildings

Híjole! (EE-ho-lay)   a slang expression roughly meaning "Oh, boy!"

jarabe (ha-RAH-beh)   an early California dance named after a sweet mixed
drink known for its smoothness

mija (MEE-ha)   an endearing term for daughter, combining "mi" (my)
and "hija" (daughter)

Ole!   an exclamation meaning "Bravo!"

pueblo   a town or village

rancho   ranch

reata   a rope to tie horses or mules or to catch animals with

señora   Mrs.; lady

señorita   miss; young lady

tío   uncle

vaquero   cowboy